First published 2000 in *The Macmillan Treasury of Nursery Stories*
This collection first published 2010 by Macmillan Children's Books
a division of Macmillan Publishers Limited
20 New Wharf Road, London N1 9RR
Basingstoke and Oxford
Associated companies throughout the world
www.panmacmillan.com

ISBN: 978-0-230-74999-3

1 3 5 7 9 8 6 4 2

A CIP catalogue record for this book is available from the British Library.

Printed in China

MACMILLAN CHILDREN'S BOOKS

Jack and the Beanstalk
and other stories

Retold by
Mary Hoffman

Illustrated by
Anna Currey

Jack and the Beanstalk

There was once a widow who had one son, called Jack. He was the apple of her eye but he was an idle, thoughtless fellow. He spent his mother's money carelessly so that, in time, it ran out and they had nothing left but their one cow.

"It's no good, Jack," said his mother. "We will have to sell the cow if we are to have anything to eat. You must drive her to market and be sure to get a good price for her."

"All right, Mother," said Jack. "You can trust me."

And he set off to market with the cow. But, on his way, he met a man who had some curious coloured beans in his hat. The man saw that they had 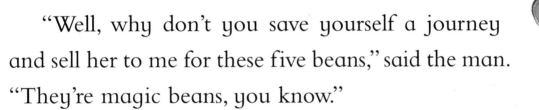 attracted Jack's attention and asked him where he was going with his cow.

"Why, to market," said Jack. "I am going to sell her."

"Well, why don't you save yourself a journey and sell her to me for these five beans," said the man. "They're magic beans, you know."

Jack thought that his mother would be glad to see him back so soon and the cow sold so easily, so the foolish boy exchanged the good milking cow for a handful of beans.

And was his mother pleased? She was not. In fact, for the first time in his life she flew into a temper with Jack and boxed his ears!

"Stupid boy!" she scolded. "Now what are we to live on? Magic beans, indeed—let's see if they fill your belly tonight!"

And she threw the beans out of the window. Jack went to bed supperless and very miserable; he was not used to being in his mother's bad books.

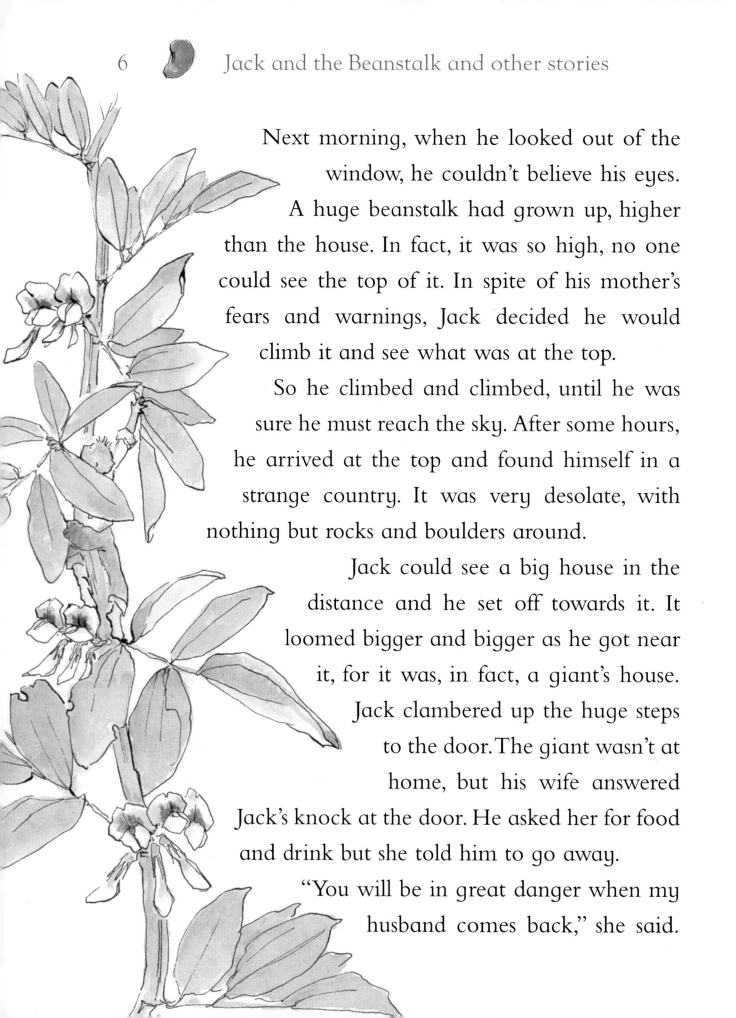

Next morning, when he looked out of the window, he couldn't believe his eyes. A huge beanstalk had grown up, higher than the house. In fact, it was so high, no one could see the top of it. In spite of his mother's fears and warnings, Jack decided he would climb it and see what was at the top.

So he climbed and climbed, until he was sure he must reach the sky. After some hours, he arrived at the top and found himself in a strange country. It was very desolate, with nothing but rocks and boulders around.

Jack could see a big house in the distance and he set off towards it. It loomed bigger and bigger as he got near it, for it was, in fact, a giant's house. Jack clambered up the huge steps to the door. The giant wasn't at home, but his wife answered Jack's knock at the door. He asked her for food and drink but she told him to go away.

"You will be in great danger when my husband comes back," she said.

"He eats human beings and he'd make short work of you."

But Jack begged and pleaded and, in the end, she let him in and gave him something to eat, and then hid him inside the stove. Just in time, for the giant was coming back and Jack could hear his mighty footsteps rumbling up the stairs.

When the giant came into the kitchen, he looked round suspiciously, sniffing the air, and said,

"Fee, Fi, Fo, Fum,
I smell the blood of a human one!"

But his wife persuaded him that it was just his supper chops he could smell. (Wasn't it lucky that she was frying them on top of the stove and not roasting them inside it?) Jack was quivering with fear in his hiding place.

The giant ate thirty-six huge chops for supper and twenty pounds of potatoes. Jack thought he would never stop. Then the giant called for his wife to bring him his pet hen. Jack couldn't believe how gentle and kind the horrible giant was to the little hen. But then she laid an egg— of pure gold! Now Jack could see why the giant was so fond of her.

It wasn't long before the giant was asleep and snoring. Jack crept out of the stove, snatched up the hen and ran out of the giant's house. He didn't stop running till he reached the top of the beanstalk and climbed awkwardly down it, with the hen under his arm.

His mother was waiting anxiously for him at the bottom of the beanstalk.

"See, Mother," said Jack. "I am not good for nothing. I have brought you a hen to replace the cow."

"Well," said his mother, "it will be good to have eggs to eat even if we have no milk to drink."

"These eggs are not for eating," said Jack, and he set the little hen gently down on the ground, where she laid an egg of solid gold.

Jack and his mother lived very well after that, selling the golden eggs. Their larder was always full and they bought themselves another cow and some ordinary hens.

But Jack could never forget his adventure up the

beanstalk, of which he had said little to his mother, as she tended to worry about him. As the months went by, he felt more and more restless and eventually he just had to go back up it again.

His mother tried to stop him, but it was no good. He disguised himself, in case the giant's wife should recognise him, and set off on his long climb.

The country was just as before and he made his way back to the giant's house and knocked at the door. The giant's wife didn't recognise him but she refused to let him in.

"Not long ago I took pity on a poor lad like you and he stole my husband's magic hen," said the giantess, "and now I never hear the end of it."

But Jack flattered and cajoled her and, in the end, she let him in and fed him and hid him in a cupboard. Not much later, Jack heard the sounds of the giant returning.

"Fee, Fi, Fo, Fum,

I smell the blood of a human one,"

said the giant, sniffing the air.

"Nay, it is nothing but the side of beef I am roasting for your supper," said the giantess.

Jack watched through a crack in the cupboard door while the giant ate the whole side of beef and three apple pies, each the size of a dustbin lid. All the time he was eating, the giant was grumbling to his wife about the loss of his hen.

After his supper, the giant called for something to amuse him and his wife brought him his sacks of money to count, which was a favourite hobby of the giant's. Jack's eyes nearly popped out of his head when he saw how many silver pieces spilled out of one sack. And then the gold coins which poured from the other! Jack

had never seen so much money. He waited till the giant was asleep and snoring again. Then he crept out of the cupboard, snatched up the sacks and staggered to the door. He was terrified that the giant would wake up, but he was too full of food. So Jack made it safely to the beanstalk and carried down the sacks of treasure.

How pleased his mother was to see him safe! And she was amazed by the silver and gold. For three years, she and Jack lived happily and prosperously. Their house now had every comfort; they ate well and slept on soft beds. They had the garden enlarged, to include an orchard and a vegetable patch.

But it was still dominated by that huge beanstalk and, in the end, Jack just had to climb it again. His mother was against it and pleaded with him not to go. But the spirit of adventure was strong in Jack.

Besides, he had grown a lot in three years and he now had a beard, so he didn't think the giantess would know him.

He climbed the beanstalk again and went to the giant's house a third time. The giantess didn't want to let him in.

"It has always ended badly for us whenever I have let a human in," she said.

But Jack was a charmer and used to getting his own way. In the end, she let him in and fed him and then hid him in the copper. Shortly afterwards, Jack heard the giant coming home.

"Fee, Fi, Fo, Fum,
I smell the blood of a human one!"

he bellowed as he came into the kitchen, his nose twitching.

"It is only the pig I am roasting for your supper," said his wife. But the giant was still suspicious and hunted round the kitchen. Jack sat shivering in the copper, sure he would be caught.

At last the giant sat down to his supper and ate a whole pig, and a cauldronful of jelly and custard. He drank a whole barrel of wine to go with it. Then he called for his wife to bring him his harp.

Now this was a magic harp which played the most wonderful tunes all by itself. Jack was enchanted by the sound of it and determined to steal this, too. He waited till the giant was asleep and snoring, then crept out of the copper and snatched up the harp.

But the harp, being magic, called out, "Master, Master!" and the giant woke up! Jack tried to run, but he was so scared he was frozen to the spot. Then he saw that the giant was too full to chase him properly. This gave Jack back his courage and he started to run.

The giant ran after him and, if he had eaten less, he would easily have overtaken him. As it was, he followed Jack to the beanstalk and started to climb down after him. Jack scrambled down as fast as he could, still clutching the harp.

He reached the ground and dashed to the garden shed for an

axe, as the beanstalk was shaking with the weight of the giant. Jack hacked at the tough beanstalk with his axe and it began to creak and sway. Then it fell to the earth, bringing the giant down with a dreadful crash. He lay stretched out dead, taking up the whole of the vegetable patch.

Jack's mother was as glad to see the end of the beanstalk as Jack was to know the giant was dead. They lived happily in the same house for years and never lacked for food again. And Jack settled down and became just the sort of son his mother had always wanted.

The Wolf and the Seven Little Kids

There was once a nanny goat who had seven little kids, whom she loved as dearly as any human mother ever loved her babies. One day she had to go into the forest to fetch some food, but she was worried about a wolf who lived nearby. So she called all her seven children to her and gave them some advice.

"My dear little kids, I must go and get us some food. Now while I am away, you must watch out for the wolf.

He is very good at disguises, but you should know him by his rough voice and his black feet."

"Don't worry, Mother," said the kids. "We will take care of one another."

So away she went. Not long afterwards someone came to the door and knocked, saying, "Let me in, dear little kids. It is your mother come back and I have something nice for each of you to eat."

But it was a harsh rough voice and the little kids bleated, "You are not our mother! She has a soft gentle voice and yours is so horrid you must be the wolf!"

The wolf went to a shop and bought himself a huge pot of honey. He ate the lot and it made his voice soft and pleasant. Then he went back to the goats' house and knocked on the door, saying, "Dear little kids, let me in. It is I, your mother, and I have something nice for each of you to eat."

But while he was talking, the wolf laid his black paws against the window and the kids cried out, "You are not our mother! She has sweet white woolly feet. Yours are so hairy and black, you must be the wolf!"

Cursing and growling, the wolf ran to the mill and told

the miller to sprinkle his paws with white flour. At first the miller said no, guessing the wolf was trying to deceive someone. But the wolf threatened to eat him if he didn't, so the miller sprinkled the wolf's paws with flour.

A third time the wolf came to the goats' house and called, "Dear little kids, let me in. It is I, your mother, and I have something nice for each of you to eat."

"Show us your feet," said the kids.

And the wolf obligingly put his floury paws on the window sill. The kids were quite convinced it was their mother this time and opened the door. Whoosh! In rushed the wolf, and the kids all scattered. One hid under the table, one in the bed, one inside the stove, one in a cupboard, one behind the woodpile and one inside the washing bowl. The seventh and youngest little kid hid inside the case of the grandfather clock.

The wolf found them all except the seventh and ate them all up.

Not long afterwards the nanny goat came home. How upset she was to see the door open, the table knocked on its side and the washing bowl broken on the floor. She ran about the house distracted with worry, calling her kids by name. But it wasn't until she called the seventh one that she heard any reply. "Is that you, Mother?" called the frightened little kid from inside the grandfather clock.

How she embraced her one remaining child, weeping as she heard what had happened to the other six. In her grief she wandered out of the house, with the last little kid trotting behind her, and strayed into a nearby meadow.

There they found the wolf sleeping off his huge meal. The poor goat saw something squirming in his stomach and thought, "Could it be that my children are still alive?" She sent the littlest kid back to the house to fetch a knife and a needle and strong thread. When he got back, the goat cut open the wolf's stomach. He had been so greedy that he had swallowed the six little kids whole! One by one they came popping out of the cut that their mother had made.

What rejoicing there was when the mother and her precious children were

reunited! The wolf slept on and while he snored, the kids found some big stones and put them in his stomach and the goat sewed him up again with the needle and thread. Then the goat and the seven little kids went and hid behind a tree to see what would happen.

When the wolf woke up he felt terribly thirsty but, as he walked towards the stream to quench his thirst, the stones in his stomach knocked together and made him feel very peculiar.

When he reached the stream, the wolf put his head down to drink and the weight of the stones unbalanced him so that he fell into the water and drowned.

As soon as the seven little kids saw what had happened to the wolf, they danced for joy, singing:

"The wolf is gone, the wolf is drowned,
The kids he ate have all been found.
The wolf is drowned, the wolf is dead
We'll eat our supper and go to bed!"

The Hare
and the Tortoise

The hare and the tortoise were having an argument over who could travel faster.

"It's obviously me," said the hare, appealing to all the other animals who were listening. "I mean, look at the size of my back legs! And I'm famous for my leaping and bounding through the fields."

"True, true," agreed the badger and the fox and the field mouse, nodding their heads.

The tortoise shrugged.

"We shall see," he said. "If you're so sure, you won't mind having a race with me."

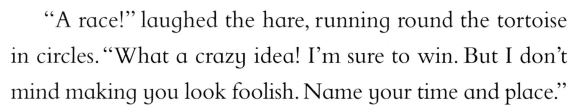

"A race!" laughed the hare, running round the tortoise in circles. "What a crazy idea! I'm sure to win. But I don't mind making you look foolish. Name your time and place."

The animals settled on a race from the big oak tree in the hedge to the elm at the corner of the field, to be held at sunrise the next day.

Next morning, the tortoise was at the oak tree bright and early and, as soon as the sun rose, he set off across the field at a steady pace. The hare, on the other hand, overslept. When he saw that the sun was already climbing high in the sky, he thought, "It will take the tortoise ages to get from one tree to the other. There's still plenty of time for me to overtake him."

And he yawned and went back to sleep. Meanwhile, the tortoise was plodding his way determinedly along the race course at about a quarter of a mile an hour.

By the time the hare woke up and got himself to the oak tree, he could see the dark hump of the tortoise's shell moving through the corn near the elm.

"Help!" thought the hare, and he put on all the speed he could with his big long back legs. But it was too late. As the hare reached the elm tree, panting with his efforts, the tortoise was already being congratulated by all the other animals on having won the race!

"But that's ridiculous!" gasped the hare. "Anyone can see I'm faster than he is!"

"Nevertheless," said the tortoise, calmly, "slow and steady wins the race."

And there was nothing the hare could do about it except go back to his den and sulk.

The Three Sillies

There was once a farmer and his wife who had a very pretty daughter. But although she was pleasing to look at, she was not very clever—and this was not surprising, for her parents were not very clever either. But this foolish pretty girl was being courted by a gentleman, who came for supper at the farmhouse every evening.

It was the girl's job to go down to the cellar and draw a jug of beer from the barrel that was kept down there. One evening, when she was doing this, her attention

wandered and she noticed a mallet wedged in the rafters above her head.

"Oh, wouldn't it be terrible," said the girl to herself, "if I married and my husband and I had a son and he grew up and came down here to draw some beer and that mallet fell on his head and killed him?"

And she was so upset by this dreadful idea that she sat down on the floor and threw her apron over her head and began to howl. After a while she was missed upstairs and her mother came to look for her. She found the beer running out of the barrel all over the floor and her daughter in floods of tears.

"Why, whatever's the matter?" exclaimed the mother.

"Only think, Ma," sobbed the foolish girl. "Suppose I got married and we had a son and he grew up and came down here to draw beer. There's a horrid old mallet up there in the rafters and it might fall down on his head and kill him stone dead!"

As soon as the mother had heard this awful suggestion, she, too, sat down and threw her apron over her head and began to cry just as loudly as her daughter.

"I can't think what has happened to the women," said the farmer. "They're taking an awfully long time to draw a jug of beer. I'd best go down and see what's keeping them."

And when he got down into the cellar, the farmer saw his wife and daughter sitting with their aprons over their heads and crying fit to bust, while the beer ran all over the floor.

"What on earth has happened?" he asked, in some alarm.

"Why, husband," wept his wife. "The most terrible thing. Look at that mallet stuck in the rafters! Suppose our daughter married her suitor and they had a son and he grew up and came down here to draw beer and that horrid mallet fell on his head and killed him!"

"That's awful!" said the farmer and he sat down beside them and burst into tears, too, at the thought of his grandson's fate. The gentleman had been left all alone upstairs and soon became anxious about what had happened to the family, so he went down into the cellar to find them.

Imagine his surprise at finding all three sitting on the floor, which was awash with beer, crying their eyes out! He stepped quickly to the barrel and turned the tap off.

"Will someone please tell me what is going on?"

"Alas," said the farmer. "Do you see yonder mallet stuck in the rafters? Suppose you marry my daughter and the two of you have a son and he grows up and comes down here to draw beer and that mallet falls on his head and kills him? Isn't that cause enough for grief?"

The gentleman could hardly speak for laughing. He went over to the mallet and pulled it out of the rafters and set it on a shelf.

"Dry your eyes, all of you. You really are the three

silliest people I have ever met! Now I am going on my travels and if I can find three people sillier than you, I shall come back and marry your daughter."

With that, he left the three sillies crying just as hard, because the girl had lost her sweetheart. He hadn't travelled far, before he saw an old woman trying to persuade her cow to climb a ladder.

"Why are you trying to get your cow up the ladder?" he asked.

"Why, I want her to eat the grass growing on the roof of my cottage," said the old woman. "It's a shame to waste it. And she'll be quite safe because when I've got her up, I'll tie this string round her neck and pass it down the chimney and fasten it round my waist."

"But wouldn't it be easier just to cut the grass and throw it down to the cow?" the gentleman couldn't help saying.

The old woman took no notice of this suggestion and the gentleman travelled on. But he heard a shriek behind him and turned to see that the cow had been hoisted onto the roof. It had slipped and fallen back down to the ground, yanking the old woman up the chimney!

The gentleman laughed so hard at the sight of the old woman on the roof all covered in soot shaking her fist at the cow, who was now munching the grass in her garden, that he nearly fell off his horse.

"Well, there is one person sillier than my sweetheart and her parents," he thought.

He travelled on and found an inn in which to rest. He had to share a room with another traveller, a very pleasant man, who was a good companion. But in the morning, this fellow-traveller did something very strange.

He hung his trousers on the doorknob, then went to the other side of the room and took a run at them, trying to jump into them! He did the same thing several times, till he was sweating with the effort, while the gentleman looked on in astonishment.

The man mopped his brow. "These trousers are the invention of the devil!" he panted. "It always takes at least an hour to get into them. However do you manage to get dressed so quickly?"

So the gentleman showed him the easy way to put on trousers, though he could hardly do so for laughing. As he went on his way the gentleman thought, "There is another person sillier than my sweetheart and her parents."

He travelled to a village where there was a crowd of people gathered round the pond, with rakes and brooms and sticks.

"What's up?" he asked one of them.

"Nay, rather ask what's down," said the villager, "for

look—the moon's fallen into the pond and we can't get it out."

In vain did the gentleman point up at the sky to show them that the moon was still there and that what was in the pond was just a reflection. The villagers didn't want to know and sent him on his way with many insults.

"Why," thought the gentleman. "There are many more sillies in this world than my pretty sweetheart and her good parents."

And he rode back to the farm and asked the farmer's daughter to marry him straightaway. Which she did, and if they are not happy still, it is not my business or yours.